PIPER GREEN *and the* FAIRY TREE: THE SEA PONY

Book

PIPER GREEN and the FAIRY TREE

THE SEA PONY

ELLEN POTTER *Illustrated by* QIN LENG

Alfred A. Knopf | Yearling
New York

THIS IS A BORZOI BOOK PUBLISHED BY ALFRED A. KNOPF

Visit us on the Web! randomhousekids.com

Educators and librarians, for a variety of teaching tools, visit us at RHTeachersLibrarians.com

Library of Congress Cataloging-in-Publication Data
Names: Potter, Ellen. | Leng, Qin, illustrator.
Title: The sea pony / Ellen Potter ; illustrated by Qin Leng.
Description: First edition. | New York : Alfred A. Knopf, [2016] | Series:
Piper Green and the Fairy Tree ; 3 | Summary: On an island off the coast of Maine, where children ride lobster boats to school, Piper wants a horse but finds, instead, another object hidden in the red maple tree.
Identifiers: LCCN 2015035219 | ISBN 978-0-553-49931-5 (trade) |
ISBN 978-0-553-49932-2 (lib. bdg.) | ISBN 978-0-553-49933-9 (ebook) |
ISBN 978-0-553-49934-6 (pbk.) | Subjects: | CYAC: Horses—Fiction. | Islands—Fiction. |
BISAC: JUVENILE FICTION / Family / General (see also headings under Social Issues). |
JUVENILE FICTION / Imagination & Play. |
JUVENILE FICTION / School & Education.
Classification: LCC PZ7.P8518 Se 2016 | DDC [Fic]—dc23
LC record available at http://lccn.loc.gov/2015035219

The text of this book is set in 17-point Mrs Eaves.
The illustrations were created using ink and digital painting.

Printed in the United States of America
August 2016
10 9 8 7 6 5 4 3 2 1

First Edition

First Yearling Edition 2016

To Sonja Philbrook,
who deosn't mind silly questions
—E.P.

To Sarah
—Q.L.

Crow
Island

Egg Island

Mink
Island
School

MINK ISLAND

MAINLAND

CHAPTER ONE

THE IMPORTANT STUFF

My name is Piper Green and I live on Peek-a-Boo Island.

There are two things you should know about Peek-a-Boo Island:

1. All the kids on the island ride a lobster boat to school.

2. There is a Fairy Tree in my front yard.

You might not believe in fairies and things like that. That's okay. Last Easter, my little brother, Leo, said he stopped believing in the Easter Bunny, because the Easter Bunny didn't hide any eggs in our house that year.

Then Mom marched into my room and found the thirty-six Easter eggs that I stashed in my underwear drawer.

Now I'm not allowed to get up at four a.m. on Easter morning anymore.

CHAPTER TWO

NECK CANDY

The first thing I did that Saturday was stare at my fingernails.

"You look very splendid," I said to them. "You especially," I told my left thumb.

Each fingernail had a tiny purple snail with a white swirl on it. My aunt Terry painted them when she visited yesterday.

I hopped out of bed, pulled on some clothes, and ran down the hall to Erik's room. He's my older brother. During the week, Erik lives on the mainland and sleeps in his school dorm. That's because there is no high school on Peek-a-Boo Island or any other islands close by. He comes home almost every weekend, though. This weekend, Mom was working at the health clinic, Dad was fishing on his lobster boat, and Leo was at his friend's house. That meant I had Erik all to myself.

Erik was snoring, with his head under the blanket.

I sat on the edge of his bed.

"Erik?" I whispered.

"Unnngha?" he muttered.

"Look at my nails, Erik." I stuck my hands under the blanket. "Aren't they gorgeous?" I wiggled my fingers. "Hey,

I just thought of something! They're not fingernails. They're finger SNAILS!"

"Hnnn."

"Okay, soldier"—I patted what I thought was his head—"get ready for action! First we are going to make tin-can stilts and stomp all over the house. Then we can go to the mudflats and find some clams—"

Erik threw the blanket off his head.

"Not today, Piper. I feel lousy. I think I have the flu or something."

I looked hard at his face.

"What?" he asked.

I pointed at a pimple on his chin. "That's a fresh one."

He groaned.

"I know what will make you feel better really quick," I told him. "Cinnamon snakes. Whenever I'm sick, Mom makes them for me and I always get better the next day. Since tomorrow is Sunday, we'll still have time to do all our fun stuff."

Cinnamon snakes are not real snakes, by the way. They are just cinnamon, sugar, and butter on bread, which Mom cuts into squiggles.

Erik closed his eyes. "Sure. That sounds good."

I ran out to the kitchen, but two minutes later, I was back in Erik's room.

"There's only one problem," I told him. "We're out of cinnamon."

"Okay." He put the blanket over his head.

"Don't worry, though. I'm going to go to the Little Store and buy some," I told him.

He didn't say anything.

I took the blanket off his head.

"So can I have some money?" I asked.

He looked at me with his aggravated face. He pointed to his jeans on the floor. I took out three dollars from his pocket.

"I'll be back before you know it," I told him, and I put the blanket over his head again.

Before I went to the store, though, I made a quick stop at the Fairy Tree. The Fairy Tree is a fat red maple tree at the end of our yard. First I made sure that none of its branches were broken after last night's storm. They all looked A-okay. After that, I scrambled up the tree and sat down in the nice, cozy crook next to the hole in the trunk. That's where the fairies leave treasures for me. Except first I have to leave one for them, which I did yesterday.

"I hope you liked my purple nail polish," I said.

I thought for a minute.

"I also hope fairies have fingernails."

Before I reached into the hole, I took a deep breath. If there's one thing I've learned about fairies, it's that you never know what the heck they will put in the Fairy Tree. One time, they left me two kittens, which I named Glunkey and Jibs. Another time, they left me just one earring. My neighbor Mrs. Pennypocket says that the fairies don't always leave things that you *want*. Instead, they leave things that you *need* . . . even if you don't know that you need them.

I reached into the hole and felt around in there. My fingers touched something cold and smooth. I scooped it up, took it out, and looked at it.

It was a necklace! At the end of a chain was a long, thin pendant made of slippery-smooth *gold*!

"Ooooh!" I cried out. "Neck candy!"

That's what Aunt Terry calls a necklace.

I'd never had a fancy necklace before. The only necklace I owned was made out of folded-up potato chip bags. My best friend, Ruby, made it for me.

I put the necklace around my neck. The

chain was so long that it reached my belly button. I held up the backs of my hands so that my finger snails could see it.

"Nice, huh?" I said to them. "Plus, it doesn't even smell like barbecue flavor."

CHAPTER THREE

THE LITTLE STORE

The Little Store is right across from the wharf. It's a pink building with a green sign that says "Peek-a-Boo Island Grocery Store." But everyone just calls it the Little Store. You can't believe how much stuff is crammed into that tiny place! Milk and eggs and bread, but also hammers and nails, flashlights, aspirin, bait bags, paint, rope, whoopie pies, soda, ice cream, Band-Aids, and little wooden lighthouses.

"Well, good morning, Miss Sassy-Pants,"

said Mrs. Spratt, who was arranging boxes of tea on the shelf.

"Hi, Mrs. Spratt. How do you love my new necklace?"

Mrs. Spratt knelt down to get a better look at it. Then she did the weirdest thing. She picked up the pendant and put it in her mouth.

"Hey!" I yelled. "It's not a chicken finger, lady!"

Mrs. Spratt blew right into the pendant, and it went, *PHWEEEEEE!*

"Whoa! How did you make my necklace do that?" I cried.

"Because it's not a necklace. It's a whistle.

Look." She held it up and showed me the hole that you blow through.

"Wow!" I put it to my mouth and blew. *PHWEEE! PHWEE-PHWEE!*

"It's called a bosun's whistle," Mrs. Spratt told me. "It's a special brass whistle they used to have on ships to send messages to each other. It was made really loud so that people on the ship could hear it in bad weather."

Oooh! A talking whistle!

"Guess what *this* means," I said. Then I blew it as hard as I could.

PHWEEEEEEEEEEEEEEE!!!

Mrs. Spratt jumped a little.

"It means I need cinnamon," I told her.

"Aye, aye, Captain," said Mrs. Spratt.

She found a little container of cinnamon on the shelf and brought it over to the checkout counter. I handed her Erik's money, and she gave me back the change. She also gave me a lollipop that was root-beer-flavored, which I love, and a piece of bubble gum.

I stuck the little container of cinnamon in my right pocket and the bubble gum in my left pocket. I was going to eat the lollipop, so I held on to that.

Then I picked up my whistle to thank her.

"No need to thank me!" she said quickly, holding up both hands.

But I thanked her anyway.

PHWEEEEEEEEEP!

The store's door opened, and old Mr. Mathers walked in. I waved and blew a special hello whistle for him. I made it kind of soft and shaky-sounding, like his voice. He smiled and waved back. Then he picked up a loaf of bread and brought it to the counter.

"There's an awful big crowd of folks out there waiting for the ferry to come in," said Mrs. Spratt, peeping out the store window.

"Ayuh," said Mr. Mathers. "I hear there's something special on board today."

"Really, now?" said Mrs. Spratt as she gave Mr. Mathers his change. "What is it?"

Mr. Mathers shrugged. "No one seems

to know. Everyone is on pins and needles waiting to find out."

I wondered what it could be. A candy-vending machine, maybe? Or a gigantic turtle?

Then I thought of something.

"I bet it's a CIRCUS!!" I said in my whistle language.

The whistle must have shouted this, because Mr. Mathers dropped his change all over the floor.

That's when Mrs. Spratt said that my whistle might be more of an "outside whistle."

Which is code for: "It's time for you to leave."

CHAPTER
FOUR

EXTRA-SPECIAL
DELIVERY

Holy cow, there really *was* a big crowd waiting for the ferry! It seemed as if most of
the island was standing out there.

I looked around until I spotted my
friend Jacob. Too bad I also spotted
my not-friend Allie O'Malley standing
with him. She was wearing a headband
with red-sequined Minnie Mouse ears,
which she got from Disney World over
the summer. Jacob and Allie were both
watching the big white ferry coming into
the harbor.

"Guess what the ferry is bringing, Piper?" Allie O'Malley said when I walked up to them. "Presents! Presents for everyone on the island!"

"No one knows what's on the ferry, Allie," Jacob said.

"Well, *I* think it's presents for everyone," she told him.

"You wish, jellyfish," I said in whistle talk. "Anyway, I think it's a circus." Then I put my whistle down and gave my lollipop a lick.

Allie squinted at me. Then she squinted at my whistle. "What on earth are you doing with that thing?" she asked.

I put my whistle back to my mouth and

blew out, "Talking to you, Allie O'Malley. Obviously."

It sounded like *PHWEEE-PHWEE PHWEEP PHWEEP, PHWEEEPY PHWEEP PHWEEPY. PHWEE PHWEEPY.*

In the harbor, the water whooshed loudly as the ferry came in. The crew put the metal gangplank into position. First, the cars that were on the ferry drove down the gangplank. Then the passengers walked down the gangplank, carrying bags of groceries and dragging coolers on wheels.

"Can you see anything?" Allie asked, standing on her tiptoes and stretching her neck up.

"Nope," said Jacob.

Suddenly there was the sound of *clackety-clackety-clackety* against the metal ferry floor. Then we saw it, walking across the deck. A horse! Which is the exact thing I have always wanted for my entire life!

It was a dark brown horse with a white stripe down its nose. Its mane was shiny black, and its tail was so long it almost touched the ground. A man was holding it by a rope and leading it toward the gangplank.

There were lots of oohs and aahs. That's because there were zero horses on Peek-a-Boo Island.

"I wonder who it belongs to," said Jacob.

I wished with all my heart that it belonged to me. I imagined sitting on that horse's back and galloping all around town. I might even ride with no hands when I passed Jacob's house so that I could amaze him.

"I'm going to get a horse," I whistled.

Allie fluttered her eyelashes at me in a disgusted way. "No one knows what you're saying, Piper."

"Jacob understands me," I whistled, looking at him. "Don't you, Jacob?"

PHWEEP PHWEEEP, PHWEE PHWEEP?

Jacob thought for a minute.

"I bet she's saying that she wants a horse," he said.

"Horses are expensive, Piper," Allie

said in her smarty-pants voice, "and your family isn't exactly rolling in money."

Allie O'Malley's dad owns the biggest, fanciest lobster boat on Peek-a-Boo Island. I imagined the O'Malley family rolling around the living room floor on piles and piles of dollar bills. Mrs. O'Malley would have dollar bills stuck in her hair. Allie's little sister, Wanda, would probably eat the money, because she eats anything that's on the floor. She once ate her own baby wipes.

"My dad said I might get a pony when I turn double digits," Allie said. "Maybe I'll let you ride my pony once in a while, Piper . . . *if* you are a little more mature by then."

I blew my whistle at her. This time my whistle didn't say anything, though. I just felt like blowing it at her.

Allie put her hands on her hips and turned to Jacob. "She's being ridiculous, as usual."

"I know you are, but what am I?" I whistled.

Allie turned back to me and shook her head. "You are so weird, Piper."

"And you are a BAG OF SMELLY TOENAILS!!" I said this in my loudest whistle voice.

It turns out that loud whistles make horses jumpy. Because, all of a sudden, that horse started stomping its feet

against the metal gangplank and shaking its head.

"Who is blowing that darn whistle?" asked the man who was leading the horse.

That's when I snuck away.

CHAPTER FIVE

CINNAMON SNAKES

I know Mrs. Pennypocket said that the Fairy Tree gives you stuff you really need. But the only thing that the whistle seemed to do was get me into trouble. And I don't need any help doing that.

I kind of wished I had my purple nail polish back.

Suddenly I had a great idea!

I ran up the road and back to the Fairy Tree as fast as I could. I climbed up to the fairy hole and gave the tree trunk a friendly pat.

"It's me again, guys," I said to the fairies. "So I was thinking . . . if you want to give me something that I *really* need, you should give me a horse. Because a horse would come in handy during emergencies. Like if Mom ran out of milk or something, I could just jump on my horse and ride to the Little Store and get her some."

On second thought, that didn't seem like too much of an emergency.

I put my chin on my knee and I thought a little more. I tapped on my forehead, because that's how you knock some sense into your brains.

Then I got it!

"Another emergency might be if Mrs. Snortingham is choking on a Brussels sprout."

Mrs. Snortingham is a pig. She belongs to Nora Bean, who owns a farm all the way on the other side of Peek-a-Boo Island.

"And what if Nora Bean calls Mom for help? A horse would really come in handy then, right? I could gallop Mom straight over to Nora Bean's farm, top-speed, and Mom could pull that Brussels sprout right out of Mrs. Snortingham's mouth."

I took the whistle off my neck. "So I'll just be tucking this old whistle right back in here," I said as I put the whistle into the fairy hole.

I took the piece of bubble gum out of my pocket and put it in the fairy hole too.

"That's just a little extra bonus for you guys," I said. "Now I'm going in the house to make some cinnamon snakes for Erik. I'll be back out here soon, so you should probably get busy."

I ran to the house to make Erik's cinnamon snakes. I took out a slice of bread and a stick of butter from the fridge. With a butter knife, I cut off a hunk of butter and started to spread it on the bread. But that butter was very frustrating. It just wouldn't smooth down on the bread. I punched it a couple of times, which helped a little. Then I dunked a spoon in the sugar bowl and

poured sugar all over the bread. After that,
I sprinkled on the cinnamon. I punched it
all down some more. Now it was time to cut
it into squiggly snakes. I was pretty excited
about this part. Except all that punching
had made holes in the bread, so the snakes
came out too short. They looked more like

cinnamon worms. Plus, they were flattish, which made them look like worms that someone had stepped on.

I put them on a plate. I tried to arrange them in a nice way so that they didn't look as disgusting. Then I carried the plate to Erik's room. But guess what? That kid was still snoozing! The side of his face was mashed against the pillow, and his mouth was wide open.

How was he going to get better by tomorrow if he didn't eat the cinnamon worms?

I cleared my throat a few times. Then I made some monster noises. But he just kept on snoozing.

I knelt down next to his bed, and I carefully put one of the cinnamon worms in his open mouth.

"Chomp, chomp," I whispered in an encouraging voice. But Erik's tongue pushed that cinnamon worm right out of his mouth and onto the pillow.

I put the cinnamon worm back in his mouth. His tongue pushed it out onto his pillow again, but this time he rolled over on it. I could see a smoosh of butter and cinnamon in his hair.

"Hmm," I said, looking at the mess in his hair. "I guess I'd better just let you get some sleep."

Then I tiptoed out of there.

CHAPTER SIX

STERNMAN PIPER

After that, I went outside to check on my horse situation. I walked all around the Fairy Tree. I peeked behind our dogwood bushes. I looked in the shed.

But darn it, because I didn't see a horse anywhere.

Maybe the fairies left him somewhere else, I thought. *And maybe there's a note in the tree to tell me where he is.*

I ran back to the Fairy Tree and climbed up to check inside the hole. I patted all around in there. No note. But the fairies took the bubble gum, because that was gone. The only thing in the fairy hole was that dumb whistle. I put it around my neck again, because it was better than nothing.

"Hi, Piper."

I looked down, and there was Dad, dressed in his shiny orange oilskin pants and big black rubber boots. "Is your brother up yet? Uncle Mack wasn't feeling well this morning, and I could use Erik's help on the boat."

"Erik's not feeling well either," I told him.

"Hmm." Dad put his hands on his hips and squinted up at me. "What are *you* doing?"

"Nothing. Except for not getting a horse," I said.

He looked at me funny for a second. Then he just ignored what I said about the horse and asked, "How'd you like to be my sternman today?"

The sternman is the guy who stuffs dead fish into little net bags to use for lobster bait.

I LOVE being sternman!

Except for the dead-fish part.

Suddenly I had a new idea about how I could get my horse.

"I bet I can stuff the bait bags faster, now that I'm seven," I said to Dad. "So maybe you can pay me to be sternman."

Dad thought about that for a second. "Fair enough," he said. "How about ten cents a bag?"

I thought about that. If I stuffed the bags extra fast, faster than I ever had in my entire life, I might be able to make enough money to buy a horse. It would have to be a little horse, though, because a big horse would cost more.

"Deal!" I told him.

CHAPTER SEVEN

A WICKED BAD GULLYWHUMPER

We walked down to the wharf, and Dad helped me into the skiff, which is a little boat that you take to get to your lobster boat. Except something strange was going on.

"Hey, wait a minute!" I said. "This isn't our skiff."

This skiff was a plain aluminum rowboat. Our skiff is bright blue and it's shaped like a banana. We've had it for as long as I can remember. It's practically a member of our own family.

"Remember that storm we had last night?" Dad asked.

I nodded. "It was a wicked bad gully-whumper."

That's what my mom calls a big storm.

"It was," Dad agreed. "In fact, it was such a gullywhumper that our skiff broke free of its moorings and was swept away. I'm borrowing this one until I buy a new one."

Oh no! Poor old blue skiff! I thought about it getting tossed around in the storm in the middle of the night. Now it was all alone, lost in the big wide ocean. My heart felt achy.

"We have to look for it, Dad," I said.

"I looked for it all morning," he replied.

"But did you look *everywhere*?"

"Everywhere I could think of. I'm afraid it's a goner."

You know what I really can't stand?

I really can't stand gullywhumpers.

Dad rowed us out to our red-and-white lobster boat, the *Tiger Shark,* which was moored in the harbor. He tied up the rowboat to the mooring, and then he lifted me inside the *Tiger Shark.* Our lobster boat is not very big, and she's not fancy, like the lobster boat Allie O'Malley's dad owns. But Dad says the *Tiger Shark* reminds him of me . . . very loud and fast as a rocket.

Sometimes the ocean is full of bumpy waves. Today, though, it was flat as a plate as Dad steered the *Tiger Shark* out of the harbor. I took a big gulp of air. It tasted like salty pennies.

"Ready to get to work, Piper?" Dad called back to me.

"I was born ready, boss!" I said in a deep voice.

That's the way I talk when I'm sternman.

I picked up a little red net bag out of a barrel. Then I reached into another barrel and pulled out a dead fish. Quick as anything, I put that slimy fellow into the bag. Then I picked up another dead fish and

stuffed it in the bag too. I kept on stuffing at lightning speed till the bag was full.
I yanked down the plastic ring that closed
up the bag and dropped it in another barrel. Then I started stuffing a new bait bag.

My poor finger snails were probably
passing out from the stink.

"Hey, Dad?" I called, over the roar of the boat's motor.

"Yup?"

"Someone on Peek-a-Boo just got a horse," I told him.

"No kidding?" he said.

"I'm not kidding. And so guess what I decided to save up my money for?" I said.

"A gerbil?"

"No. A horse. I already have ten dollars in my piggy bank. And I just made ten cents more."

"I hate to break it to you, pal, but horses cost at least a thousand bucks."

"A thousand bucks!"

"Often more than that," he called back.

"Hmmph," I said grumpily.

Because a thousand bucks is a lot of *ka-ching*. By the time I stuffed enough bags to make that much money, I'd probably be an old lady with clip-on teeth, like Grandma Green.

CHAPTER
EIGHT

MYSTERY
TREASURE CHEST

Floating on the water all around us were lots of colorful lobster buoys. The lobster traps sit on the bottom of the ocean and are attached to the buoys by long ropes. Some buoys are red and green, some are blue and white, some are pink and yellow . . . every color combination you could imagine. Lobstermen paint their buoys their own special colors so they can find them on the water.

Our buoys are painted yellow and black. They look like giant bumblebees.

Dad stopped the boat. He picked up a long pole with a hook on the end and grabbed the rope attached to one of our bumblebee buoys. Then he put the rope on a machine called a pot hauler, and the pot hauler pulled our lobster traps right out of the ocean.

I almost cheered up about the horse situation, because looking in the lobster traps is my favorite part of being sternman. You never know what's going to be in the traps. There might be lobsters. But there also might be pinchy crabs or starfish or prickly sea urchins or funny-looking sea cucumbers. It's like a mystery treasure chest from the bottom of the ocean.

Dad pulled up two traps. There was one greenish brown lobster in the first trap. A lot of people think that lobsters are red, but they're not. They only turn red when you cook them.

Dad measured the lobster to make sure it wasn't too big or too small. Then he turned the lobster over to check if there were any eggs on its belly. Nope. He also checked to see if its tail had a little notch in it. The notch means it's a lady lobster, who can have babies. If the lobsters are too big or too small, or if they have eggs or a notch, you have to throw them back in the ocean.

"This one's a keeper," Dad announced.

With special pliers, he put thick rubber bands around the lobster's claws and then placed it in a barrel of water.

We looked at the second trap. Jackpot! There were five lobsters. There was also a purple starfish, an eel, and a gigantic rock crab. Dad picked up the crab and quickly tossed it in the water before it could pinch his fingers. I picked up the eel. I wanted to get a better look at it, but it was so slithery that it slipped right out of my hands and back into the ocean. Then I picked up the purple starfish. Its little legs curled around my hand as if it was hugging me. I love the soft, nubbly feeling of starfish.

I petted it carefully with one finger. Then I leaned over the rail to put it back in the water very gently.

That's when I noticed two big brown eyes looking up at me.

CHAPTER
NINE

THE SEA PONY

I gasped inside my head. My mouth stayed very quiet, though.

Because those big eyes belonged to a seal's face! The seal was gray with lots of spots all over and long whiskers.

"Well, hello there! Are you looking at my finger snails?" I wiggled them for him. "They're not real snails, see, so don't even think about taking a bite out of them." The seal's nose twitched. "Oh! I think I know what you want. Don't move a muscle. I'll be right back."

While Dad was busy putting bands on the lobsters, I went to the bait barrel. I pulled out the fattest fish I could find. I did it sneaky-style, though, because I didn't think Dad would want me to waste any bait. I tossed it to the seal. He caught it right in his mouth and chomped it up.

"Did you like that, cutie pie? Was that yummers?" I said in baby talk.

Then I remembered I was a sternman, so I cut that out.

Dad started up the motor again, and the *Tiger Shark* hurried off to the next traps. The seal bobbed in the water, watching us leave. He looked as if he was sorry to see me go.

"So long!" I called out to him.

But the motor was roaring, and the bubbly wake was *shoosh*ing behind us loudly. I didn't think he could hear me. Then I remembered Mrs. Spratt saying that a bosun's whistle is so loud it can even be heard in bad weather. I reached into my shirt and pulled out my whistle.

"So long!" I whistled to him.

PHWEE-PHWEEE!

You'll never guess what happened. Right after I blew the whistle, the seal dove underwater. A few seconds later, his head popped up by the boat, and he swam right alongside, staring up at me.

I quick snuck a couple of fish out of the

bait barrel and tossed them to him. He gobbled them up and then swam away.

I whistled again.

PHWEEEEEEEEEEEEEE!

Splish! Up came his head right by our boat.

"You're a smart cookie," I told him.

I fed him a few more fish.

"Hey, I have a great idea!" I said. "You could be my pet seal! And I'll call you . . . hmm . . . how about Scoot? Do you like that name? Scoot? And whenever I blow my whistle, you can come see me, okay?"

I ran to the bait barrel and grabbed up a bunch more fish for him.

Just then, Dad cut the motor, and we

stopped next to some of our bumblebee-colored buoys.

"I just thought of something else," I told Scoot. "I could ride on your back! It would be just like having my own pony, and you don't even cost a lot of *ka-ching.*"

I imagined riding on Scoot's back while he swam around the harbor. I'd hug him tight around his neck, and we'd swoop up and down on the waves. Maybe I could even ride him to school. I pictured Allie O'Malley's surprised face when she saw me on Scoot's back, riding alongside the school boat, waving to her. That made me smile.

"I guess those fairies knew what they

were doing after all," I said to Scoot. "They didn't leave a pony, but they gave me a special whistle that brought a pony to me!"

"Who are you talking to?" Dad asked.

"Scoot," I said, and pointed at Scoot. He had swum away from the boat and was bobbing in the water, watching us from a distance.

Dad looked at Scoot. He made his eyes narrow and suspicious. Then he went to look in the bait barrel.

Uh-oh.

"Piper," Dad said to me in his angry voice, "have you been feeding our bait to that seal?"

"He's a sea pony," I muttered.

"You are seven years old, Piper," Dad said. "Seven's not a baby anymore. Think! What would happen if I fed my bait to all the seals? Hmm?"

"You wouldn't catch any lobsters," I mumbled.

"That's right. And no lobsters means no money. You've wasted half my bait today, Piper, and we can't afford to do that, especially now that I have to buy a new skiff."

"But I wasn't feeding *all* the seals, Dad," I said. My eyes were getting teary and my mouth felt wobbly. "I was just feeding one *special* seal."

Dad looked at me and sighed. I think some of his mad left his body with the sigh.

"All right, Blue Eyes," he said to me. "Let's hear it. What's so special about this seal?"

"For one thing, I love him. And also, when I blow on my whistle, he comes." I picked up my whistle and gave it a good *PHWEEEEEEP!*

Scoot dove under the water, and the next minute he was right by the boat.

Even Dad looked surprised.

"See?" I said. "Isn't he a smart cookie?"

I leaned way down, over the rail, to pet his slickery head.

And that's when the terrible thing happened.

CHAPTER
TEN

THE TERRIBLE THING

The chain on my whistle slipped right off my neck and into the water.

"Oh! OH NO!" I cried.

But before I could grab it back, Scoot poked his nose through the chain. The next thing I knew, that sea pony was wearing my whistle around his neck.

I leaned farther over the rail and stretched out my hand, but I couldn't reach him.

"Scoot! Come here, boy!" I said in an encouraging voice.

Scoot stayed right where he was, staring at me with his big round eyes.

"Scoot, you bring me my whistle!" I ordered.

But I guess Scoot wasn't great at following orders, because that's when he decided it would be fun to swim in the other direction.

"Follow him, boss!" I shrieked at Dad.

"Piper, it's just a whistle—"

"It's a special whistle! It's a . . . a . . . a sea pony whistle! If I lose it, Scoot will never come to me again!"

Dad looked at me as if I had lost my marbles, but I made such a fuss that finally he said, "All right, all right, keep your hair on."

He went to the wheelhouse and put the boat in gear, and we started moving again. But we weren't going fast enough.

"Is that all you got? Step on it, boss!" I yelled.

Dad looked back at me with a cranky face.

I tried to keep my hair on after that.

The *Tiger Shark* began picking up speed. Scoot swam and swam while we raced after him. We chased him all around Tom Thumb Island, then past Blueberry Cove. The boat's engine was roaring, and the wind was whooshing in my ears. I was glad that the *Tiger Shark* was small and speedy!

Every so often, Scoot would dive under

the water and disappear. But right when it seemed as if we had lost him, his shiny dark head would pop up again.

In front of us, I could see Little Gull Island, where we once went with Grandma and Aunt Terry for a picnic. Suddenly Scoot stopped swimming. His head disappeared under the water, and when he came up again, my whistle was not around his neck anymore.

"Oh no!! It's gone! My whistle drowned!" I wailed.

"No it didn't!" Dad yelled over the sound of the motor. "It's right over there!" He pointed, and I saw it, floating on top of the water.

"Oh yes, I see it!" I shouted back.

Dad slowed the *Tiger Shark* down. When we were close to the whistle, Dad stopped the boat. Then he went to the stern and, leaning over the rail, scooped up my whistle and handed it to me.

"Thank you, Daddy! Thank you, thank you!"

I tried to toot an extra-loud "thank you," but the whistle sounded as if it needed to clear its throat. I held it over the rail and gave it a good shake to get the water out.

That was when I spotted something. It was stuck on a sandbar near Little Gull Island. It was bright blue and shaped like a banana.

"Dad!" I shouted, and pointed. "There it is!" I was so excited I could hardly get the words out of my mouth. "It's our skiff!"

Dad looked. Then he put the edge of his hand above his eyes, as if he thought the sunlight was playing tricks on him.

"Well, how about that!" he said, smiling. "I would never have thought to search for it here. And the skiff doesn't even look worse for wear. We can tow it back right now." Dad nodded at me. "Nice work, Sternman."

"If it wasn't for Scoot, we wouldn't have found it," I reminded Dad.

"I guess that's true," Dad said. He went to the bait barrel, took out three fish, and then tossed them to Scoot. "You earned this fair and square, buddy!"

CHAPTER ELEVEN

A KNOCK ON THE DOOR

Guess what we had for supper that night? Cinnamon snakes! Mom and I made them for everyone, and I didn't even have to punch the butter this time. It turns out that after you put the butter and sugar and cinnamon on the bread, you stick the whole thing in the toaster oven to melt it. It would have been a perfect supper, except that Mom also made me cut up carrot sticks for a side dish.

While we ate, Dad and I told everyone

all about Scoot and my whistle and the missing skiff.

"Cool bosun's whistle," Erik said. He had just finished his fifth cinnamon snake, and he was already looking healthier.

"It's not a bosun's whistle," I told him. "It's a sea pony whistle."

"What's a sea pony?" asked Leo.

"Scoot's a sea pony," I told him. "Because I'm going to train him to give me rides on his back."

Everyone got quiet. Mom and Dad slid their eyeballs to each other, which is what they do when they are both thinking something they don't want to say out loud.

Leo picked up Harold, who was stuck to the table next to him.

Harold is a yellow Post-it note.

Leo held Harold up to his ear for a minute.

"Harold says that you can't train a seal to be a pony," Leo told me. "He says it's impossible."

"It's *not* impossible," I said, "because Scoot is very intelligent. And, FYI, Harold is a slob, because there is tomato sauce all over his face."

Leo licked his finger and tried to rub the tomato sauce splotches off Harold, but it only turned them into spitty pink smudges.

"Remember, Scoot's a wild animal, Piper," Mom said.

"I know that," I said. "But whenever I blow my whistle, Scoot comes to me. The whistle is so loud, Scoot could hear it even if he was way out at sea. Listen."

I picked up the whistle from my neck and took a big breath. Then I gave the loudest blow I could.

PHWEEEEEEEEEEEEEEEEEEEEEEEEEP!!!

Everybody squinched up their faces.

I took the whistle out of my mouth and said, "See what I mean?"

Suddenly there was a knock on the door.

Everyone's eyes got wide. Mine included.

Then Leo leaned over and whispered to Harold, "If that's the sea pony, I am going to freak out."

CHAPTER
TWELVE

LOLA

I jumped out of my chair, ran to the door, and flung it open.

"Whoa!" I said under my breath.

A huge, hairy head ducked down and poked its nose through the door. Its nostrils blew out a puff of warm air right in my face.

"A pony! A really *real* pony!" I said.

I put out my hand and petted its silky mane. The pony made a little snuffling sound.

Then I had a crazy thought.

"Wait a minute. Are you *Scoot*?" I asked it. I looked carefully into the pony's big brown eyes. "Did you turn into a real pony?"

"Helloooo down there!" said a voice.

"Wait . . . can you talk?" I whispered in shock to the pony. "Because that would be awesome!"

"Anyone care for a ride?" the voice asked.

"That sounds like Nora Bean," Mom said. She, Dad, Erik, and Leo had come up behind me to see who was at the door.

The horse took a few steps backward. Now I could see that it *was* Nora Bean, the lady who owns Mrs. Snortingham. She was sitting on the horse and smiling down at me.

"That's the horse from the ferry!" I cried out. "The horse belongs to *you*?"

"That's right," said Nora Bean. "Her name's Lola. And as horses go, she's the finest kind." Nora Bean patted Lola's neck. "Your dad said you might be interested in some riding lessons, Piper."

"Really?" I looked at Dad.

"It would have cost me a pretty penny to replace that skiff," Dad said. "Since you were the one who found it, Piper, I figured you ought to get a reward. I'm trading Nora Bean two lobsters for each riding lesson."

"The lobsters aren't for me," Nora Bean said. "Frankly, I don't even like lobster. They're for Mrs. Snortingham. She's just crazy for lobster."

"Thank you, thank you!" I said to Dad. I threw my arms around him, and he squeezed me back.

"First lesson starts now," said Nora Bean.

We all went outside. Nora Bean hopped off the saddle. She shortened the stirrups so my feet could fit into them. Then she helped me up onto Lola's back.

I felt like a giant up there!

"Did you know that the top of your head is shaped like a sweet potato, Dad?" I said.

"I do now," Dad said.

"I'll lead Lola with the reins, Piper," said Nora Bean, "and you hold on to her mane. Go ahead. She won't mind."

I grabbed some of Lola's mane. I was careful not to pull, though, because I hate it when Mom yanks too hard on my hair when she puts it in a ponytail.

Nora Bean led Lola back down our front path. *Clackety-clackety-clackety.* I rocked from side to side. It felt like keeping your balance on a lobster boat when the water is choppy, which I am a professional at.

I thought about what it would be like to ride on Scoot. The ocean would be pretty cold. And Scoot's back looked slippery.

Maybe he made a better seal than a sea pony. Next time I was sternman, I'd save the biggest fish in the bait barrel for him. I bet Dad wouldn't even get mad about that.

At the end of the yard, we turned onto the road. We walked right by the Fairy Tree. I almost whistled, "Thank you, fairies!" but then I remembered that whistles make horses jumpy. So I gave the Fairy Tree a thumbs-up instead.

"Hey, Nora Bean?" I called down to her. "Can we swing by Allie O'Malley's house? I want her to see this."

"I think we can manage that," said Nora Bean.

"Good," I said. "And then after that I

want to ride by Jacob's house, because I am going to amaze that boy."

Then I let go of Lola's mane and held my hands way up in the air.

THE END

ABOUT THE AUTHOR

Although she doesn't ride a lobster boat to work, **Ellen Potter** can look out her window and see islands, just like the one Piper lives on. Ellen is the author of many books for children, including the award-winning Olivia Kidney series. She lives in Maine with her family and an assortment of badly behaved creatures. Learn more about Ellen at ellenpotter.com.

ABOUT THE ILLUSTRATOR

Qin Leng was born in Shanghai and lived in France and Montreal, where she studied at the Mel Hoppenheim School of Cinema. She has received many awards for her animated short films and artwork, and has published numerous picture books. Qin currently lives and works as a designer and illustrator in Toronto.

LOOK FOR PIPER'S NEWEST ADVENTURE!